With simple words and bold illustrations, author-artist Taro Gomi playfully takes us through the four seasons. With a turn of the page, a calf's back becomes a sprouting garden. Another turn of the page transforms a snowy landscape back into the calf. By toying with color and perspective, the artist coaxes the reader to look carefully at each illustration and to look with renewed imagination at the everyday world around us.

". . . the artist's playful approach to perspective makes this a perfect picture book."
—*Publishers Weekly*

". . . pure colors, bold shapes, and whimsical touches are more than enough to engage young minds."
—*Booklist*

"Thoughtfully designed, the book is a consistent entity, an artfully simple, artistically logical execution of a basic concept."
—*Horn Book*

"These large, uncluttered illustrations and minimal text make this an ideal choice for toddler story time as well as one-on-one usage with the lapsitting crowd."
—*School Library Journal*

WINNER OF THE BOLOGNA GRAPHIC PRIZE

First published in the United States in 1989 by Chronicle Books.
© 1989 by Taro Gomi.
American text © 1989 by Chronicle Books.
First published by Libroport Co., Ltd., Tokyo, Japan.

Printed in Hong Kong.

Library of Congress Cataloging-in-Publication Data

Gomi, Taro.
    Spring is here / text and pictures by Taro Gomi.
    32p.   20 x 25.4cm.
    Summary: Text and pictures take us through a year of seasons beginning when spring arrives and a calf is born.
    ISBN 0-8118-1022-4 (pb.)
    ISBN 0-87701-626-7 (hc.)
    (1. Seasons—Fiction.) I. Title.
    PZ7.G585Cal 1989
    (E)—dc19
88-39848

CIP

AC

Distributed in Canada by Raincoast Books
8680 Cambie Street, Vancouver, B.C. V6P 6M9

10 9 8 7 6 5 4 3 2

Chronicle Books
275 Fifth Street
San Francisco, California 94103

Spring is Here

Taro Gomi

chronicle books

San Francisco

Spring is here.

The snow melts.

The earth is fresh.

The grass sprouts.

The flowers bloom.

The grass grows.

The winds blow.

The storms rage.

The quiet harvest arrives.

The snow falls.

The children play.

The world is hushed.

The world is white.

The snow melts.

The calf has grown.

Spring is here.

TARO GOMI attended the Duwazawa Design School in Tokyo. Since his graduation in 1966, he has been involved in a variety of design areas, ranging from animated cartoons to children's clothing. He has illustrated more than one hundred books for children, garnering him many awards.